SOME DADS...

Scholastic Canada Ltd.
604 King Street West, Toronto, Ontario M5V 1E1, Canada

Scholastic Inc.
557 Broadway, New York, NY 10012, USA

Scholastic Australia Pty Limited
PO Box 579, Gosford, NSW 2250, Australia

Scholastic New Zealand Limited
Private Bag 94407, Botany, Manukau 2163, New Zealand

Scholastic Children's Books
Euston House, 24 Eversholt Street, London NW1 1DB, UK

Typeset in Euphorigenic and Geist Serifa.
Nick Bland used acrylics on paper to create this artwork.

Library and Archives Canada Cataloguing in Publication

Bland, Nick, 1973-

        Some dads-- / written and illustrated by Nick Bland.

ISBN 978-1-4431-1387-8 (bound).--ISBN 978-1-4431-1388-5 (pbk.)

        I. Title.

PZ7.B557Som 2012   j823'.92   C2011-907560-1

First published in Australia by Scholastic Press, 2011
This edition published in Canada by Scholastic Canada Ltd., 2012

Copyright © 2011 by Nick Bland

6 5 4 3 2   Printed in Canada   114   12 13 14 15 16

SOME DADS...

nick bland

Scholastic Canada Ltd.

Toronto New York London Auckland Sydney
Mexico City New Delhi Hong Kong Buenos Aires

There are some dads who **worry**.

And some dads who

huRRy.

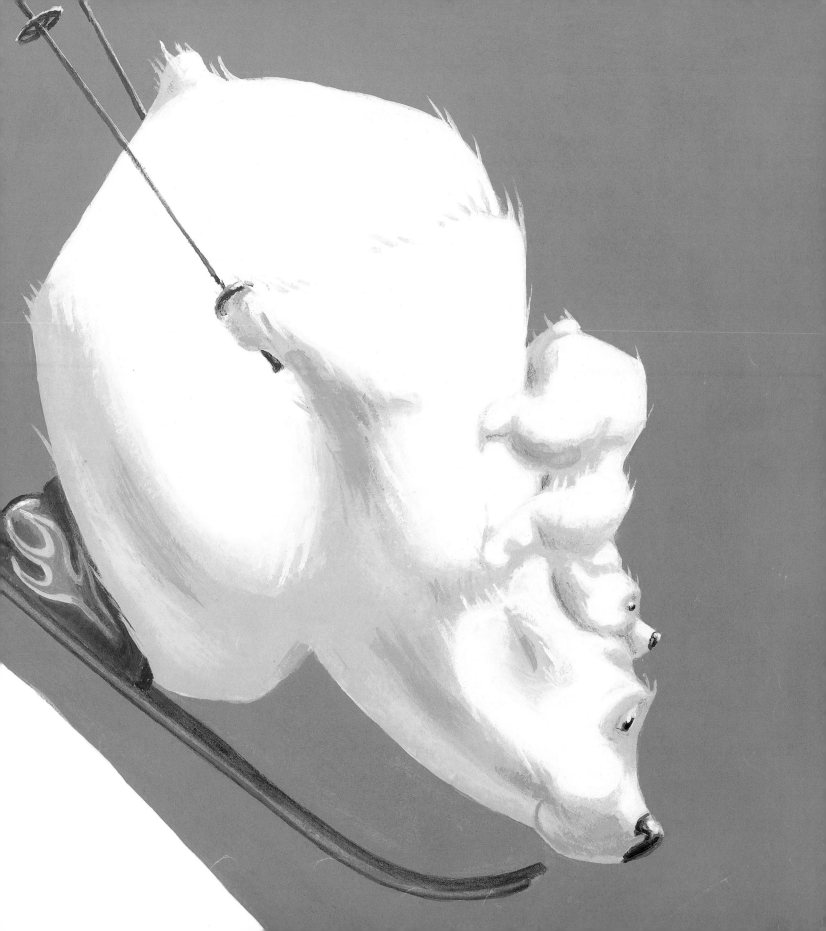

And some dads who get lost on the way.

Some dads are sporty.

And some dads are **naughty.**

And some dads just brighten your day.

Some dads like **strolling.**

And some dads
rock 'n' rolling.

And some dads just love the outdoors.

Some dads are
loud.

And all dads are
proud.

And you'll never forget
which is yours.